Incubus Dreams: Complete Collection

Incubus Dreams

Cassandra Vayne

Published by Knotted Quill, 2021.

INCUBUS DREAMS: COMPLETE COLLECTION

First edition. January 21, 2021.

ISBN: 979-8201954932

Written by Cassandra Vayne.

Also by Cassandra Vayne

Incubus Dreams
Incubus Dreams: Part 1
Incubus Dreams: Part 2
Incubus Dreams: Part 3
Incubus Dreams: Part 4
Incubus Dreams: Complete Collection

Standalone
Good Boy
Fylgja
The Inheritance
Prey
Ink and Pom-Poms
A Flash of Scale
Trail Run
Forest's Patience: A Paranormal Lesbian Romance
A Dance for the Warlord

Table of Contents

Part One

Chapter One

'*I can't believe it worked.*' Allison thought. When she found the dusty artifact on a back shelf in the basement of the museum, it seemed impossible. When she translated and read the spell, it seemed impossible. When the pale, naked man with orange eyes and a tail appeared from the shadows, his member swollen and ready for her, she still thought it impossible.

"I am Velis. How may I service you?"

Even when he spoke, Allison doubted what she saw in front of her. When those slit pupil eyes sparkled with amusement and full lips turned into a dark grin. He stood taller, combing his dark hair with his clawed fingers. "You disbelieve? So many do. Well, if you are going to doubt your senses, you may as well doubt them all." Velis swooped in, claiming Allison's lips and pressing her hand to his burning prick. He devoured her mouth, fangs nipping, tongue tangling fearlessly as he used her hand to stroke himself.

Allison moaned as the biggest cock she'd ever touched squirmed in her hand. Surrendering completely to the taste of opium on the incubus' tongue. Her knees buckled, panties soaked, a surrendering moan poured from her throat. Velis wrapped his tail around them both, locking them together to allow his hands to make short work of her clothes. The prim suit jacket and skirt were thrown to the floor, revealing the creamy breasts and swollen flesh between her quaking thighs. Allison found herself laid down and spread open in a bed of her own clothing, the lithe creature only abandoning her lips to hear the gasps from the throat of his prey.

"Open for me, pretty one. Beg me to take you." Velis caressed Allison's aching nipples, smiling against her gleaming wet lips as he teased her with the hardness of his shaft in her hand. He thrust against her palm, her knuckles trapped against her dripping sex. "You must invite me, pretty one or I cannot service you."

"I need you to take me right now." Allison growled, raking her claws over the alabaster skin. She spread her thighs in an impressive display of flexibility, clear framed glasses fogged with the dew of her passion sweat.

'*No hesitation. Lovely...*' Velis purred as he pushed into her, the soaked folds parting easily around his cock. He immediately employed his arsenal of tricks, rolling his spine and snapping his hips to bring the mewling female to orgasm. He fed off her moans, her dripping cooze, and bucking desperation as she cried out for relief. Licking her long throat, he felt her ecstasy rise to its crest, felt it seep into his skin and nourish him. This mortal was a sweet meal, so innocent yet demanding and needy. Too soon would he feed from her and be returned to his stone prison to await a new master to feed, fuck, then leave to wait to be summoned again. He would have vanished before he could even spill the last drop of his seed.

'*But no matter.*' Velis groaned, singing his song of bliss along with the thrashing woman beneath him. He could feel her passion rising as he fucked her harder, her juices splashing shamelessly between them and dripping down to stain her clothes. Allison's cries grew louder, screaming out his name. He could taste the very crest of her lust, feel it rising and fueling his own. The ache in her pussy echoed in his balls and he angled his thrusts to bring her tumbling over the edge.

Instead of the expected cry of release to herald his own, Allison let out a heartbreaking cry of frustration as she was filled, Velis grunting as she clutched him tight as if in pain. Her climax was snuffed out and her emptiness bled into every cell in Velis' body.

"W-what-"

"That's why I summoned you." Allison panted through eyes burning with angry tears. "I can't orgasm."

Chapter Two

"I-I don't understand..." Velis stammered, frozen in place with his seed leaking from Allison.

With angry tears in her eyes, she shoved the baffled incubus back and snatched up her clothes. "I cannot orgasm. I am unable to cum. Can't climax. Denied the 'little death.' Take your pick of euphemisms but it all adds up to everybody getting fucked but only me unsatisfied."

Velis landed bonelessly on his ass, heedless of the abrasive concrete on his bare flesh. "How is this possible?"

"I have no idea. But trust me, I have a string of frustrated partners and thirty years of my own frustration to present as evidence." Allison tugged her hair back into its bun and pushed the clear framed glasses back up her nose.

"I have never left someone unsatisfied." Velis started to shake, clinging to himself so hard his claws dug into his skin. "Never."

Allison looked at the stunned demon with pity. "Trust me, it isn't you. It's me." She lifted the stone artifact in her hand, the chipped obelisk nestled in her palm. "If you can't help me, I guess nobody can. You might as well go home."

"You don't understand." Velis looked up at her like a lost puppy. "If you are not satisfied, I cannot go home. You cannot even release me from your service till you orgasm by my hand."

"You're trapped here?" Allison paled and lost her grip on the stone. Velis snapped out of his shock and darted to catch it before it hit the floor.

"Yes." The demon stood, sighing as he placed the obelisk back into Allison's shaking hand. "But if you break this, I will never be able to go home. As charming as this world is, I don't exactly blend in." Flicking his tail for emphasis, Velis cocked his hip and slowly dragged his hand from hers to raise goosebumps on her arms. "And if you cannot feed me, I will starve and waste away." With a calculating grin, he purred; "Unless you can feed me others..."

Instead of swooning as others did, Allison bristled, pulling her hand away and turning her back on the naked creature. "Of course. Why not. Everybody gets to come but old Alli; she of the broken vag."

Velis tilted his head, a comically innocent expression of curiosity from a creature who oozed debauchery from every pore. When he first was summoned, he thought her frustration was typical of any mortal who would feel the need to summon a demon. But it was soul-deep, strangling her spirit and leaving her pussy swollen in a constant state of arousal. Velis could relate, his member twitching to relieve the ache of his summoner.

"What is your name?"

"Allison." She whined, running her eyes over the artifact and then the swelling demon's equipment.

Velis preened under the attention. "I will remain till I have satisfied you but I shall remain until I am certain you can climax uninhibited. However," Velis licked his lips. "If you cannot feed me, you must find me others. I cannot help you if I am not at full strength."

Allison raised a severe eyebrow and forced herself to look Velis in the eye. "I give you willing women and you'll find a way to make me come?"

"Women, men, and everything in between; makes no difference to me." The demon shrugged, his tail flicking happily behind him. "Do we have an agreement, Allison?"

Her hands clenched at the way he said her name; sinful promises dripping from every syllable. "Yes." She croaked.

"Good girl."

Chapter Three

Even smothered in Allison's formless trench coat, Velis attracted the gaze of every person with a pulse and returned a lascivious look or wink every time. Allison blushed at the attention, thinking about how much of a shameless slut he was but as a demon whose very life depended on getting laid, she couldn't fault him. With a comically large fedora balanced to cover his horns, what should have been the look of a creepy flasher was sex repackaged on the strutting incubus. Allison was very grateful Velis kept pace with her hurried strides to her car lest an orgy break out right on the street.

"I'd tell you to lay down in the backseat but I think you'd cause more attention with your hard-on sticking up in my rearview mirror." Allison grumbled, unlocking the passenger side door.

"I cannot help what I am." Velis said, sinking into the passenger seat. When Allison slid in beside him, he continued; "But don't be jealous. I can climax yet I always hunger. You hunger yet cannot climax. We are two of a kind."

Allison's face softened but she said nothing; allowing the incubus to watch her as she drove. It was rare to have the chance to see the mortal to which he was bound, Velis served his summoner's needs and went back to his totem only slightly aware of their body and his hunger slaked for a few moments. This latest female he could study, memorize the soft planes of her round face, the dark rings under her hazel eyes from too many hours spent staring at a computer screen, the daring curves of her body hidden under prim suits, and auburn hair squeezed tight in a severe bun. He thought back to the moment where that body trembled close to the peak, gleaming with sweat and meeting his hips with enthusiasm. Such a shame such a willing body, ripe and silken soft, was unable to feel the heights of pleasure he could easily bestow upon others.

Velis licked his lips, suddenly dry as heat and hunger made his member swell anew '*I shall certainly enjoy my attempts.*' He thought.

Allison made no conversation the entire drive, which didn't bother Velis one bit. The nature of his occupation didn't allow him much time in the mortal world so to see such sights as cars and busses, and towering buildings after so many centuries of hurried fucking was a feast for his eyes. He was almost disappointed when Allison pulled up to her small Ranch style home and invited him inside.

"It's not much, but it's mine." She sighed.

"You live here alone?" Velis pulled off the fedora the moment the front door was closed and tossed it onto the blue couch.

Allison looked at Velis strangely, more shocked by the demon trying to get to know her than his existence as a whole. "Yeah. No roommate, no siblings, both parents gone, and no boyfriend sticks around cause what man wouldn't take it personally when he can't make his girlfriend come?"

"Hmmm, more's the pity for them." Velis removed the trenchcoat with the flourish of a stage magician. "They gave up far too soon."

Allison shuddered, backing up as Velis advanced upon her. "T-they tried everything."

"Everything a *human* man could do." Velis kept coming, a satisfied grin blossoming on his face when his prey fell back onto her couch. "Just let me work, Allison."

She nodded and the lithe creature slithered between her legs, pushing the blushing female deep into the cushions. Velis made a show of smelling her, drawing his breath in deep as the proper pencil skirt drifted higher on Allison's thighs. Her sensible shoes fell to the floor and Velis' clawed fingers danced up to the waistband of her pantyhose. The sticky scent of their last coupling still clung to her thighs and made his member pulse, bumping against the seam of a wayward pillow.

Velis pressed his nose against the damp cleft as his claws pulled at the pantyhose, only lifting his face to pull them completely off of her left foot. With a final leer, he buried his face in the dampening folds, lapping teasingly over the fabric. He could still taste the remnants of their last coupling and the thought of the swollen flesh marinating in sin all this time was enough to inspire a growl from the eternally hungry incubus.

Allison mewled, fisting the pillows and mashing her aching mound against his face. Her knees spread wider, desperate for more. She ached to feel what his tongue could do; to feel it against her swollen flesh and wiggling inside her. She moaned at the thought and the sound swelled into a wail as Velis swirled his tongue over her clit through her panties. It was all so good, but too little to tip her over the edge even if she could finally fall.

Then Velis filled her hole with his tongue, wriggling deep inside her with preternatural length. Allison dug her nails into his scalp as she felt the tongue fill her deeper than anyone or anything has ever penetrated her.

"W-what are you doing?" Allison stammered as she writhed under him.

The togue withdrew and Velis looked up at her from between her knees. He licked his lips and grinned as her juices glistened on his chin. "We shall try an endurance test first. Perhaps no human could withhold long enough to provide you with relief. Now, I shall see if an incubus' stamina can withstand your affliction." Velis dove back in, his tongue penetrating deep and swelling to fill her. The wet appendage rolled and stretched, pressing against every inch inside her.

Allison trembled and rocked her hips into his face. "Oh, fuck. I'm so close! Don't stop!"

Velis growled, vibrating her clit before leaning back and stroking her thighs. "Not yet, my pet. I'm going to keep cresting you until you can't help but explode."

But an hour later, Velis was left curled up in Allison's sweaty lap. "I can't believe it." He gasped, now trembling himself with hunger. "My tongue has never failed anyone before."

Allison stroked his head. "It's not you, remember?"

Velis sighed. "I made you a vow and I shall keep it. But I will need to be fed before we can continue."

Hearing his breath whine, Allison frowned. '*I didn't think he could get so weak.*' She patted his shoulder. "I have some food if that will help while I figure something out?"

He lifted his head and sat up, his face still dumbstruck. "That will be helpful for now."

Allison smiled. "You can use my shower while I get it ready." She watched him tottle off to her bathroom and only followed him to grab her robe and raid the fridge. '*I wonder who'd be okay with this. It's not exactly a normal request.*' She sipped at a glass of water while some leftover Chinese food spun in the microwave. '*I've met some crazy people trying to come. I bet one of them can help.*'

Part Two

Chapter One

Allison tapped her fingers on her desk, scrolling through on the mouse when the results on the screen proved useless. The unexpected bonus to being in charge of cataloging and organizing various museum artifacts was ending up with a lot of time alone with a computer. Her particular affliction left her no choice but to be devious and diligent about her internet history, performing some impressive feats with various apps and the browser's questionable anonymous feature to keep her activities secret from work.

'I need to feed.' Velis' voice echoed in her mind. Perhaps one of the contacts Allison accumulated from her search for true release could help.

All these years of frustration not only left her with dissatisfaction but a complete lack of hesitation in seeking sexual opportunities. Allison refused to use the word "slut" but in the same turn embraced her ruthless search for pleasure.

"G'morning, Ali." A voice deprived of caffeine made her jump in shock.

"Hey, Tony. What brings you down to the dungeon?"

"Hiding from the dragon man." Tony grumbled, rubbing the bridge of his nose.

Allison grunted in disgust. Nothing worse to deal with at any job than a person like Evan, who thinks they're in charge without any actual authority. Especially if you hooked up with them. "Hate to say I told you so but..."

Tony rubbed the back of his head, the fringe of his black hair falling in front of his glasses. "Unlike anyone else, I know mean that." He pulled over a chair and fell into it with a groan. "You were the most chill hookup I've ever had. Even if it didn't work out."

Thinking back, Allison clenched her thighs at the thought of Tony tirelessly working over her, so generous with his hands and tongue... Bless him, he'd tried his best to make her orgasm. Bless him further for being one of the few partners to not take it personally and lash out against her. "I wasn't kidding when I said 'it's not you, it's me.' You were amazing but I'm broken somehow."

"Yeah, you said that." Tony fumbled around his bag for his tumbler, scuffed and scratched from multiple hits to the ground and sessions in a dishwasher. He took a long drink, counting on the scalding temperature to aid the coffee in waking him up. "He had me on the phone until 3 am cycling between screaming threats and begging for another chance. Then God forbid I be a second late today. I'll have a fun appointment with HR once I get enough sleep to put two words together."

"Better make sure you get to them before Lee does." Allison leaned back in her seat and pushed her glasses up her nose; crossing her legs at the ankle and tapping her sensible heel on the floor.

"Oh please." Tony yawned. "Email with screenshots already sent. Another on the pile, according to them. Off the record, of course."

She couldn't help but laugh, the echo of the otherwise empty archives. "Came all the way down here to tell me that and hide?"

"And to complain. But you look like you missed out on some sleep, too. Hot date?"

"In a way." Allison rubbed her hazel eyes and clicked to see more results on the screen, her lips turning down. "More of the same results."

Tony left his thermos on the desk and scooted closer to hug Allison. "I know this sucks. Just be careful out there. The last thing I want is my work wife ending up with some psycho."

"It's different this time." Allison sighed and nervously smoothed her hair despite its perfection. "I found someone that I think can help me but he needs satisfaction in the meantime."

Tony gave her a look that would have made his super traditional Japanese dad proud and his Hispanic mother roll her eyes in a glorious display of exasperation. "Seriously? You've been burned by guys like this before."

'And girls.' Allison thought but the thought of Velis' coal-black eyes and dripping cock kept her from the bitterness expected from her situation. "It's different this time."

"We'll see." Tony patted her shoulder and met her eyes. "Before you do anything, let me meet him. If he's a scumbag, you back off. Deal?"

She picked at her lip, hugging herself. "Only if you meet him with an open mind, ok?"

"How open?"

"Discount store on Black Friday type open."

Tony laughed and poked Allison in the side right where he knew it would make her squeal because it tickled. "You think you're gonna shock me? Cute."

"Well, how do you feel about horns?"

Chapter Two

After a long and dusty day handling a new batch of artifacts in the basement of the museum, Tony and Allison went to their separate homes to clean up the dust of work with the promise of meeting up later.

"Velis?" Allison dropped her bag on the couch and hung her coat by the door. "Are you alright?"

Hearing no answer, Allison peeked into her bedroom to see a bundled lump in her bed that groaned at her call.

'Better not disturb him. I'll jump in the shower before Tony gets here. Better to be clean for the inevitable awkward introduction.'

The routine of undress, slippers, towel, and toilet as the shower warmed felt calming in contrast to what was to come. It has been a long time since she felt this nervous about any sexual encounter. Allison let the stream of water relax her, the steam filling the room and settling around her like a comforting blanket. Allison left her bobby pins and hair ties by the sink and she sighed as she roughed up her hair before brushing out the dead strands. She felt her scalp release the tension of the day before stepping into the shower.

Her muscles relaxed and she sighed in relief as the dust of the day slid off her body. That new shipment of artifacts to be cataloged took the entire day to organize but it all will be ready for next month's exhibit.

Except for one particular statue.

"Allison." A purr from the other side of the curtain made her jump. "I missed you all day."

"You were asleep when I got home. I didn't want to wake you."

The curtain opened and Allison scolded herself for bothering to cover her body. What part of her had Velis not seen?

"Feel free to wake me if you are naked." Velis slithered into the shower with her and wrapped her in his arms, pressing his hard cock against her ass. "You feel so good."

Panting, Allison arched into the hot rod. "But you know I can't-"

"Shhh. Just a little." Velis cupped her breasts and pinched her nipples, rolling them gently between the pads of his fingers. "To tide me over."

Allison felt the heat rise in her body and she moaned. "I think I found someone." She rasped, reaching around to cup Velis' ass and squeeze.

"Did you?" He rewarded her with a nip on her ear lobe. "Kiss me, sweet one. Let me sip at your lust."

"Will that work?" She panted, rolling her hips to feel his dick slide against the crack of her ass.

"For now, sweet one; until your 'someone' can feed me."

"I'm sorry-" Allison was cut off by Velis' hot tongue filling her mouth. Although she did not orgasm, they shuddered together as he drank what he could of her. Neither was satisfied but Velis felt stronger and Allison's desire went from a wild roar to a hot smolder.

"Better." Velis slid his hands down her soft belly and gave her neck a long lick. "You were saying?"

"I think I found someone willing to feed you." She panted, trying to ignore Velis' wandering hands as she continued washing. "He's pretty open-minded and a good friend."

"Have you been with him?" Velis kissed the back of her neck before sinking his soapy claws into her hair.

"Y-yes." Ali let her eyes drift closed as the incubus massaged her scalp.

"Never hesitate, sweet one. You will never face harsh judgment from me; nor should you from anyone."

She only groaned in response as he rinsed out her long auburn hair.

"And when will my meal arrive?"

"In a few hours. We had a rough day with some dusty new artifacts. I bet he wanted to clean up as much as I did."

"Lovely." Velis reached around to turn off the water and watched Allison secure her robe with a disappointed frown to his lips when her curves were no longer free to ogle.

Allison tossed him a towel. "There's no way I'm letting you tease me that long again."

"Not this time, dear one. I am willing to wait."

Chapter Three

Waiting turned out to be harder than she expected. "I haven't felt this nervous since I lost my virginity." Allison let her knees bounce and tried to keep her fingers from drumming on her wine glass.

"What is there to be frightened of? You know this man. You have been friends with him long enough for him to be aware of your affliction and accepts you as you are." Velis stretched out next to her, laying his head on her lap to keep her knees still.

"Yeah, he's great like that but you're forgetting a couple of things." She stroked her fingers down the curve of one of his horns.

"Ohhh, do that again." Velis mewled, his tail flicking back and forth in bliss.

Allison smiled and obeyed, thinking how strange things have become now with a naked demon purring in her lap. "Don't forget you were brave enough to summon a demon. Meeting one of your former lovers hardly compares. And I can change my form to suit my meals. I will look like whatever he finds most pleasing."

"You never changed form for me." Allison mused, taking another sip of wine as she continued to stroke Velis' horns.

The demon grinned wide, sharp teeth glistening in the light and slit pupil eyes glittering with mischief. "I didn't need to."

The door chime sounded before Allison could ask anything more. "Best to just rip the band-aid off right away." She hesitated at the door. "Are you going to put anything on?"

Velis rolled over onto his belly, his tail still flicking in amusement. "I hardly see the point."

"You might scare him off."

"I doubt that, lovely."

Allison took a deep breath and opened the door. "Hey, come on in."

Tony fidgeted with his jacket. "Do I look alright? I wasn't sure what we were doing."

Smiling, Allison gestured to her body. "We're just hanging out. I picked out my nice sweats."

"I can tell. There are less holes." Tony laughed and stepped through the threshold and out of the cool evening. "So, when will your friend get here -"

Allison shut the door then bumped into Tony's back, looking around his shoulders to see Velis, still naked and beckoning them both with a look that was positively... Coquettish, her too smart for his own good father would say.

"Hello there, Tony. I've heard lovely things about you." Velis slid to his feet and sauntered up to the dumbstruck man. "Don't be nervous. Would some of Ali's wine help?"

Tony made a croaking noise and Allison pressed a fresh glass into his hand.

"Take a sip." Velis' hand glided up Tony's wrist and brought the glass to the stammering lips. A small drop escaped down his chin. "Careful there." Velis swooped in and licked it away, traveling to slip his tongue into the warm mouth.

"I'll just take this and be over there." Allison rescued her carpet from the teetering glass of wine from Tony's hand, leaving Velis to feed in privacy. Draining her glass, she left the empty one in the sink and stole Tony's to take with her in her retreat to her bedroom.

"Not so fast." Velis hissed, the deep base in his voice making her turn and press her thighs together. "This may be my meal, but you are dessert. Stay."

Allison obeyed, sitting on the couch and leaving the glass on a coaster just in case her hands shook as well.

"Good girl."

"Uhm, I'm not sure." Tony stammered.

Velis cupped Tony's crotch and gasped. "Ohhh, I can see why Allison asked for your help. Very nice." The sound of the teeth of the zipper parting rang out like firecrackers and Velis licked his lips in preparation for the delicious meal to come.

Tony looked down and met Velis' eyes; appearing sapphire blue set on a dark-skinned, rounded face with long lashes and red bow lips. The horns were gone and replaced with short, curly hair. He ran his fingers through it and Velis sighed and leaned into the touch.

"You are so sweet." The voice coming from the demon's lips vacillated between overtly male and female as soft hands released Tony's cock and caressed the hot shaft. The bright smile of the tanned man Tony saw at his feet "Are you ready?"

"Yes." Tony croaked, widening his stance to make sure he didn't fall.

Despite appearing in a different form to Tony, Allison could see Velis' tail curling up to help his hands pull Tony's pants aside and fully release the hot cock and balls to Velis' tender mercies. The long tongue slithered over the head, collecting a drop of pre-cum from the tip.

Velis felt his very being pulse with Tony's heartbeat, ready to feed on the human's ecstasy. he took the throbbing shaft deep in his throat, working it to milk more delicious spunk from the groaning man above him. The desire built and Velis bobbed his head faster. He was too famished to draw out this encounter too long.

When Tony gripped his head in both hands and came down his throat with a gasp, Velis felt his body swell with power and strength. His pale skin took on a pinker hue and he sighed with relief. "Much better."

"Whoa..." Tony's legs nearly gave out from under him but Velis caught him and led him to the couch. "I've never finished that fast before."

"Don't worry," Velis continued undressing Tony and gave Allison a sly grin. "We are far from done."

Before either could second guess his plan, Velis stroked Tony's cock back to life and pushed his tongue between Allison's lips for her to savor the familiar taste of her friend. She felt her already rapid pulse quicken further and her nipples hardened in her soft bra. Both were worked to excitement and panting within minutes, hands throwing clothing to the floor and reaching for whatever heated flesh available.

Velis took his time now, coaxing them both to further ecstatic heights but holding the crest. He felt renewed with every moan of both pleasure and frustration from his partners but remained committed to his mission. Velis maneuvered Allison between them, delighting in watching them kiss and fondle one another. Tony was marvelous with his mouth, coaxing sweet mewls and delectable drippings from between her legs to feast on.

"Alli?" Tony whined.

"Oh, fuck yes. Do it." Allison positioned her dripping slit at the heat of Tony's cock and he rammed home, making her scream out in pleasure. Velis drank in their lust, rutting against Alli's ass before slipping one finger inside her. When she tensed, Tony slowed and Velis soothed their frustration by petting them with his free hand.

"Relax for me, sweet ones." Velis purred as he stretched Allison to prepare her. "Let us see how far we can go."

The incubus prepped her with expert care, teasing the tight ring of her anus open to ready Allison for his shaft. She opened beautifully, trembling and squirming for more and taking Tony to the edge; squeezing his cock in her dripping tunnel.

When Velis entered her, both of his morsels cried out in bliss making his skin vibrate with joy. "Match my pace, Tony." Velis hissed, thrusting forward to hear them sing for him again. "We want to make this fun."

Chapter Four

After the third glass of water, Tony slept draped in Velis' lap while the demon played with his hair. Allison stepped out of the bathroom after another shower in a different set of comfy pajamas and carrying a blanket.

"That was a bust." Alli draped the blanket over Tony and refilled her glass of wine with whatever was left in the bottle.

"For Tony, yes indeed." Velis tapped his tail on the floor as he smiled down at the sleeping man. "But despite not meeting our goal, I believe I have sensed something about you. Perhaps I can reach out to one of my friends on this side of the veil."

Allison blew a raspberry and indulged in a long sip of her wine.

"Tut tut, sweet one. Have a little faith."

Part Three

Chapter One

"There's no way you're leaving me out of this." A freshly showered and caffeinated Tony only took in the news of Velis' identity well because it was clear to him Allison had no fear of this strange creature. He was shocked, of course, but didn't run screaming into the street.

"A sweet gesture." Velis wiggled into a pair of Allison's jeans, his skin now glowing with health. Her clothes still hung loose on his thin frame as they were meant for Allison's curvy hips and large breasts. "But I can assure her safety. After all, I am in her service and she has been patient and kind." Velis shrugged on a t-shirt. "A luxury I am not frequently afforded."

Tony didn't pry but still had some reservations.

"You took the fact he's an incubus ok but here's where you're hesitant?" Allison giggled, ruffling her fingers through Tony's hair. "It's the horns, isn't it? You know, if you stroke them just right-"

"Now, delicious one. Don't betray my darkest secrets." Velis made a dramatic show of fainting into Tony's arms. The demon held his own weight by wrapping his arms around Tony's shoulders. The incubus leered up at the dark-skinned man and flicked out his forked tongue. "How vulnerable to rampant ravishing you leave me; utterly helpless to your every dark desire."

"If you keep this up, we'll never get to see your friend." Allison pulled on her coat and grabbed her large tote bag, the obelisk wrapped in a thick towel to protect it from any damage. "If your friend can help me, there'll be plenty of time to celebrate."

"Where are we going, anyway?" Tony followed after her while Velis pranced along, emboldened by the thought of tasting Ali's first orgasm.

"There is a succubus I know with a witch for a partner. Her human stumbled on her summoning object, like you, and we never learned why she never came home. She was one of the first I knew of to come to this side of the veil and willingly stay. It was speculated the witch was powerful enough to trap her here but I know her. She would never allow herself to remain if she didn't want to."

"Are you sure it's not the same problem you have?" Allison sighed, shooing both men out and locking the door.

"My dear, you are wholly unique." Velis wrapped his arms around Allison, giving her neck a greedy sniff. "And far from a problem. A puzzle perhaps but not a problem."

"Down, boy. Get in the car." Alli poked the tip of Velis' sharp nose. "Both of you." She pointed the same fingertip at a blushing Tony.

They all piled into Allison's car, Velis lounging lasciviously in the backseat while Allison followed his seductively growled instructions.

"Can he do anything without sounding like sex incarnate?" Tony pumped the window control for the cool air to calm the pure lust pulsating from the backseat.

"Try taking a shower. That'll answer your question." Allison winked at Tony with a blush on her olive cheeks, making the dusting of freckles on the bridge of her nose glitter among the red flush.

"It is my nature." Velis purred, running the tip of his tail along Tony's neck to make him shiver.

"Hey, focus on giving me directions." Allison checked her mirrors and the street before pulling out of her driveway.

Velis behaved for most of the ride as he directed them from the suburbs to the city proper. The streets became thin and disorganized compared to the formal grid around it. Allison was forced to park and walk the remaining distance with her companions.

"Don't worry about a ticket. Nobody ever gets a ticket if they are patrons of this place." Velis lead the way through flying litter, oblivious to the cold wind forcing Tony and Ali to huddle into their coats.

"This place is sketchy. I'm glad I came along." Tony muttered, looking around at every suspect shadow.

"Yeah," Allison sidestepped some flying trash and kept her elbow close to Tony's. "But I know Velis would never let anything happen to us."

"Of course not." Tony coughed when the wind went up his nose. "We're his meal ticket, right?"

Allison laughed and bumped her shoulder into his. "Oh, come on. You can tell he likes us."

"Really?"

"Oh yeah." Ali licked her lips then fished her lip balm from her pocket. "Clearly, he enjoys his work but Velis could be clinical. Keep pushing that he wants to go home. But he wants to help me. Given what I've seen, I don't think he'd avoid all this trouble for a loophole he must know. We're both familiar with all the stories of tricky creatures behind some of the artifacts we catalog."

"But those aren't leading us through dark alleys at night. They weren't real."

Allison hugged her bag closer to her with half a grin. "That's true. What a world." She trailed off.

"This way, lovelies!" Velis waved to them at the top of a staircase descending into a dramatically lit storefront advertising tarot and palm readings in blinking neon. "Don't judge the decor. Hiding in plain sight works wonders in this line of work."

Allison and Tony shared a skeptical look before shrugging and moving on.

"Hello!" Velis tapped his claws on the window instead of knocking.

"We're not open until 8!" A voice called from within.

"Not for me, my dear. Tis your old friend Velis."

They could all hear shuffling before footsteps and the click of the lock. A round, heavily freckled face with a plume of coiled blonde hair appeared in the doorway. "Holy shit! Get in here, you!" Long arms pulled Velis in for a tight hug. "It's been, what, two other lives? Zinta keeps having to retell the old stories but along with some regressions, I remember that smile."

The incubus returned the embrace. "I'd know this energy anywhere. Although this body is lovely." Velis pulled back to spin the shorter woman; a slim figure draped in scarves and bangles. "Hardly the curves of the 18th century but you are as comely as ever."

"This body has some fun issues with meat and cheese, hon. Otherwise, things would probably be really different given how much I miss a good slice of New York pizza." She stepped aside. "Come in out of the cold. Who are your friends?"

"Goodness, how rude of me." Velis ushered them inside. "Blake, this is my summoner, Allison, and her good friend, Tony."

"Nice to meet... Wait, your summoner? Then, why are you still here?"

Allison blushed and Velis just smiled. "You may want to close down for the night. It's an interesting story."

Chapter Two

With the lights off outside and the theatrical costume replaced with skull and heart patterned shorts and crop top. Blake served them all tea and offered homemade apple glazed muffins while Velis explained. In the end, Blake was left tapping her flip-flop against her heel. "Velis sure took you to the right witch. And you brought his totem?"

Allison indulged in one more sip of the delicious tea blend before fishing the obelisk from her bag and handing it to Blake. "Thank you for trying to help me. I know this must be strange."

Blake smiled and placed the obelisk on the table. "Strange? That remains to be seen. Unusual? Unprecedented? Perhaps." Blake topped off Allison's tea and offered Tony another confection but he declined. "I'm guessing you've tried most of your tricks but I will need to feel or see this block to understand what it is."

"What do you mean?" Allison brushed crumbs from her mouth with a napkin.

Blake did the same then sipped at her tea. "Whatever is wrong with you is tied to this specific pleasure. You enjoyed my tea and snacks, right?"

"They were amazing!" Allison was tempted to lick the plate honestly. Was that the nutmeg? Probably cinnamon.

"And other physical contact? Hugging, cuddling, even holding hands? Any of those satisfying to you?"

"Yes. I'm perfectly comfortable with that physical contact. I can even feel pleasure but in the end, I can't, you know... Finish."

Nodding, Blake put her cup down and sighed. "Then it's directly tied to sexual release. Then I'll have to see it in action and since you might be used to these two, we need to add another push." Blake held her hand to her lips and whispered; the ring on her middle finger glowing to life.

Velis sat up in his chair, nearly scratching Blake's table. "You're calling her?"

Blake clicked her teeth. "Did you expect me to do this alone? I have no interest in this stuff. I'm sure Zinta is done feeding by now and can come help out. Two sex demons and one human should be more than enough."

"Zinta doesn't feed from you?" Tony put down his cup and leaned forward.

"Nah, I've never been interested sex. At least in this life. I don't mind if Zinta goes to get what she needs as long as she comes home to me."

Allison smiled. "They get the sex but you get the cuddles."

Blake winked a bright brown eye. "You got it."

At Tony's raised brow, Allison patted his shoulder. "I've been around, remember? I'm sure there are preferences I haven't heard of but asexual romantic is more common than you think."

"While pleasant, we cannot live on hugs alone." A silken voice poured from the shadows near the back door. The body emerged with impossible curves and bright black eyes, pale blue skin shimmering in the light. Zinta's horns didn't rise as high as Velis' but curled at the tips among her long, bright white hair.

Blake's face lit up and she jumped out of her chair with a happy squeal. "Hey, sweetie! Welcome home." She jumped into Zinta's arms, nuzzling into the taller demon's neck. "Good hunting?"

"I ate heartily but I am glad to be home." Zinta kissed Blake's forehead and looked up. "But I see we have company?"

"Yeah!" Blake broke away but pulled Zinta into her now vacant chair. "I know you remember Velis but this is Tony and Allison. Allison is the summoner but she's got a problem."

"I imagine so." Zinta accepted the fresh cup of tea Blake offered, her tail gently flicking against the chair legs. "You are well known for your satisfaction record, old friend. I would hardly expect you to be on this side of the veil for longer than a day."

"It's my fault." Allison sighed. "Since I can't orgasm, Velis can't go home."

Zinta blinked in shock, her long lashes brushing against her cheeks. "And you both see us in our true forms. How extraordinary!"

"They came to me for help, hon." Blake leaned over the back of the chair, wrapping her arms around Zinta's shoulders. "But, for me to figure out what's going on, I need to see the block in action." Blake squeezed. "Are you too full?"

Zinta's thick lips curled into a grin that made Allison's legs clench and Tony's cock swell. "I am always ready for dessert."

Chapter Three

While Blake prepared a spell circle, Tony and Allison left their clothes hung or folded neatly on a shelf near the bathroom. Allison walked into the spell area with the nonchalance of a person used to being naked in a crowd and Tony took her cue and rolled his tense shoulders to banish any remaining shyness.

Velis and Zinta waited within the circle, knowing they couldn't cross the salt barrier once it was completed without hurting themselves and breaking the spell.

Blake dusted her hands off and motioned for Allison to come over. "This will connect you to me while you're in the circle." She said, smearing warm oil over Allison's shoulders, down her abdomen, and over her thighs. "I'll be able to tell what happens when you can't orgasm and then we can figure out a way to fix it."

"Alright." Allison sighed, trying to smile.

"Hey, I know this is frustrating. But don't give up yet." Blake checked the spread of oil and the circle one final time before backing away. "Okay, everybody in the pool. And don't get too rowdy. If you mess up the circle, the feedback won't be pretty."

Velis wasted no time, devouring Allison's lips and palming her breasts. Zinta pressed the full length of her naked body against Tony's and gave his shaft a firm stroke.

"Velis spoke highly of you. " She purred licking Tony's neck. "I see he did not exaggerate."

Both humans filled the air with moans, unaware of the circle beginning to glow around them. Blake walked the edge, using a stick of chalk to draw symbols on the floor.

Velis lay Allison down on the warm floor and crawled between her knees. He groaned in bliss as he kissed his way up her thighs, savoring the taste of her skin. He placed a sloppy kiss on her clit before slithering his tongue deep inside her. Allison gasped and bucked up, only to be held in place by Velis' strong hands. His tongue worked methodically, searching out and teasing her g-spot before withdrawing to flick at her clit to drive her lust higher.

Meanwhile, Zinta had Tony spread on his back, straddling his face while she took his cock deep into her throat. She let her saliva and his precum drip down to lubricate the fingers gently rubbing at his asshole. Zinta was far more gentle with her fingers sliding against his prostate than her throat, clenching and undulating around his cock to rip desperate cries from his lips. But like Velis, Zinta refused Tony any relief, waiting for his balls to tighten and shaft to pulse before backing off to hear him whine and hiss in frustration.

The circle glowed brighter, the light spreading to the symbols and illuminating the whole room. Blake held her place at the largest symbol, rocking and humming in tune with the power all around them. Her hands were clasped together, sweat beading on her skin as the experience flowed through her.

Velis hissed and Zinta met his eyes, a plan forming silently between them. Both incubi snarled in anticipation making the humans whine out loud and the circle pulsed with power. Zinta coaxed a trembling Tony closer to Allison while Velis turned Ali around to tease his cock against the crack of her ass. Zinta had Tony turn to let Allison straddle him, sinking slowly to take him into her wet hole. Velis prepped her ass, working Allison open to take him. Allison mewled and squirmed, rocking her hips to feel more delicious friction.

As Velis slid inside to the root, Zinta spread her folds over Tony's face for him to feast on. She gasped at Tony devoured her, tail quivering with delight. Zinta held Allison as the woman trembled violently with bliss and smiled with a mouth full of sharp teeth.

"You are a lovely one. Maybe we can play more after this is done." Zinta purred and kissed Allison deeply. Allison calmed and returned the kiss with sloppy desperation.

Both males began to move, Tony taking Velis' pace to his frustration. Slowly they alternated their thrusts, making Allison cry out into Zinta's mouth. The succubus played with Allison's nipples as her ass and cunt were pleasured. Tony sank his fingers into Zinta's thick thighs as he feasted on her addictive juices. His hips thrust upwards and Allison clenched around him, making his balls tighten.

"Almost there." Velis croaked, pulling Allison up to bite harshly at her neck. Zinta took the chance to latch on to Allison's swollen nipples and flick them with her forked tongue. It pushed Allison to the brink. She hissed and screamed with frustration as the others climaxed, filling her with seed and Tony's orgasm feeding the demons.

Zinta kissed Allison's forehead as she slumped with teary eyes into Velis' arms then crawled down to lick Tony's face clean. "What say you, my love?" When she looked up, Blake was on her knees at the edge of the circle covered with sweat and tanned skin flushed. "Beloved!"

"Wait!" Blake raised a shaking hand before Zinta could injure herself crossing the circle. "I can get the broom. Just let me catch my breath."

Chapter Four

After a series of showers and stronger tea, the group gathered in a more informal setting on plush sofas and Blake in a hefty beanbag chair with Zinta hovering around her in worry. Tony sagged in his seat with Velis prodding him to eat fruit while Allison fiddled with her teacup trying to be patient.

"That's one hell of a block." Blake leaned into Zinta's arms, calmed by the contact. "And it's way beyond my ability to remove."

Allison's breath hitched and her shoulders sagged, tears budding in her eyes. "No hope then."

"Oh, honey, no." Blake didn't have the strength to reach out to comfort her but Velis sensed the need and stroked Allison's damp hair. "It's just too strong for me to break. It's not physical, it's tied to your being. No witch or sex demon would be able to break it. But that doesn't mean it can't be broken."

Velis curled his fingers into Allison's hair to stroke her scalp. "We would need to find a stronger demon."

Blake nodded. "You need to cross the veil to meet the sex demon in charge."

Zinta frowned, curling around Blake protectively. "There is no way I will allow you to attempt that today."

"I know, babe. I need to rest." Blake put down her cup and patted Allison's clenched hands. "But I will help you. Allison, whatever happened to you isn't your fault but it got you to me and I'm not gonna let you suffer."

Allison wiped her eyes and tried to smile. "Thank you."

Blake looked from her to Velis and back again. "Give me two days to gather materials and get some energy drinks. Then we're gonna take a little trip."

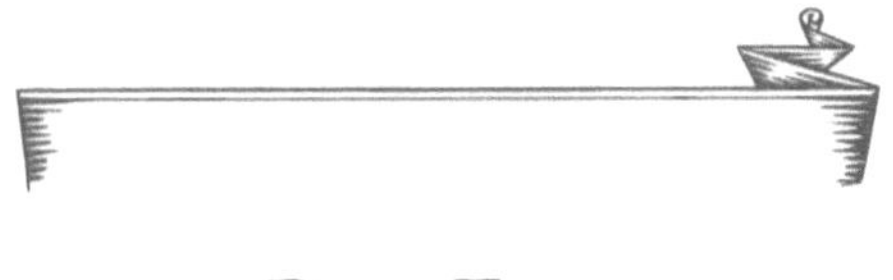

Part Four

C*hapter One*
          Allison left work after requesting a week's vacation from the bowels of the museum and went straight home to pack a bag. Blake texted her a list of possible things to pack; spare clothes, good boots, some water, and durable snacks just in case they ended up staying longer than anticipated.

"And dress for tropical-like weather." Blake had told her. "It's not what you would think of as Hell but the incubi lands are really warm."

Like their previous trip, Tony and met Allison at her house with his own bag to head out in his car to a small, disused park with enough space for a spell circle to fit all of them.

"Isn't someone going to catch us?" Tony kept glancing over his shoulders into the darkness around them. "I don't think the cops will by our story."

"The neighbors around here are sympathetic." Blake smiled, motioning for them to enter the circle. "Even if they look outside, they won't care."

"I'm not even shocked by this anymore." Allison huddled into her coat to hide her smile and pulled her hat down further over her auburn ponytail.

Velis, Ali's trenchcoat hanging off his thin frame, cuddled up close to Allison to warm her and himself. "There are such wonders in the world, Allison. A pity there is no time for me to show you."

Within the larger circle, Blake drew in intricate series of symbols and lines; leaving blank patches for each of them to stand in. By the time she was finished, Blake was out of breath and her dark skin glistened with beads of sweat. She checked her work, shaking her sore hand. "Sorry for the wait but that should do it."

Zinta shivered in her own long coat with cold and nervousness. "I have not been home in a long time." She mused, hugging her tail tight to her leg.

"While there was gossip, nobody spoke poorly of you. I wouldn't worry." Velis took his place in a blank space next to Allison and Tony went beside him.

Blake took her place in the middle and began chanting but instead of glowing bright like last time, the chalk outline turned deep red and sank into the ground an inch. Allison and Tony shivered as power hummed around them, making the air snap as if pure static surrounded them. The wind kicked up but it was warm, beads of sweat prickling the human's skin, and the incubi sighed in relief from the cold. With a few final sounds from Blake that Allison assumed were words but had too many vowels or consonants in a row for her to comprehend, the park and everything around it vanished and was replaced with a red-tinged landscape with sparse but heavily leaved trees, stone streets and distant mountains.

The circle sputtered and died, making Blake pass out into Zinta's arms. Tony and Allison swayed on their feet and Velis reached out to steady them.

"I-I'm fine." Allison felt dizzy but rapidly gained her bearings.

"I'll make sure of that." Velis winked a glittering black eye before relenting to Allison's gentle push to be allowed back on her own feet.

"Wow." Tony stripped off his heavy winter clothes for a tank he usually saved for the gym and running shorts. "I don't know what I expected but this isn't it." He gasped, craning his neck to get a better view while shoving his warmer clothes into his duffle bag.

"Amazing." Allison disrobed as well, grateful to be in warmer air as she felt the warmth chase away the chill sinking into her bones. Homes aping a modern human setting dotted the landscape in a random pattern of property sizes, vegetation growing wild and free along the streets and between the houses. The roads they landed on were meticulous cobblestones fit for the cloven feet of the natives of this world.

"Perhaps more brimstone and less crimson?" Velis chuckled. "We are far from my own home otherwise I would show it to you."

"We can't be here forever." Blake took water from her bag and gulped down half of it. "The air is made for incubi, not humans. Eventually, we'd start feeling symptoms like the bends and die."

"It is fortunate we are close to the castle." Zinta pointed to a tower a mile away. Unlike the surrounding city, the tower's architecture was more of what Allison assumed of this realm, shimmering granite, impossible angles and twisted outcrops rose into the sky from a walled courtyard.

As the group made its way towards the tower, various incubi and succubi gave them either strange looks or inciting pleas. Zinta kept composed but Velis relished the attention, bragging about his lovely human puzzle but keeping the mystery to himself. Allison was grateful to have her secret kept but not for the attention. It made the walk feel so much longer and warmer due to her reddened cheeks.

When they approached the gates, the guards with slim, muscular bodies a head taller than all of them and small wings on their backs made the group stop. "What is your business here?" The female said.

"And how did you bring humans here?" The male looked over the group, his white eyes halting on Zinta. "Ah, I see. It has been centuries, Zinta. Why have you returned?"

"She is graciously assisting me in fulfilling my duties to my summoner. And before you ask, I will only speak to our Majesty about the particulars." Velis stood in front of the group as the others waited breathlessly for a response.

"Fine then." The female said, reaching for the gate. "But be quick. Majesty will not be pleased with such a secretive disturbance."

"I am sure we will be forgiven once They hear the full story." Velis took Allison by the elbow and escorted her in with the others not far behind. They passed through sweet-smelling air from the apothecary's scented creations. Most of the light guiding them came from luminescent stones set near torches to reflect their brilliance.

Majesty sat on their throne towering above all of them and leaned forward to look closer at the group. Appraising them with white eyes set in an angular face; charcoal covered skin glimmering in the dancing light in the throne room. "Velis. Zinta. What is the meaning of this? Why are humans in our realm?"

Velis stepped forward and bowed, his inky, dark hair sliding forward to brush against the pristine floor. "My liege, my summoner has a unique riddle I must solve in order to complete my duties. You see, she is unable to climax."

Their ruler huffed, the white curls bouncing around the thick, curled horns. "A common problem any of our kind should be able to solve." They uncrossed their legs revealing a dual set of genitals. "Little cause to risk her life by bringing her here."

"It's way more than it sounds like." Blake piped up, stepping forward from the back of the group. "It's not a physical problem. We checked before risking this."

Majesty narrowed their gaze. "You are the human Zinta has followed through the ages."

"Yes, I'm a witch this time. We wouldn't have come here if we didn't think you could help her."

They stood up from their throne, thick lips drawn tight. They stretched out Their wings and crossed muscular arms over small breasts. "Show me."

Chapter Two

"I think I'm getting too used to stripping down on command." Tony folded his clothes on top of his duffel bag.

"Be careful." Allison laughed and did the same with her clothes, placing them in a neat pile on her backpack. "You might end up with a new fetish."

"Ha, ha." Tony rolled his eyes. "Seriously, this shit is fucking insane. I can't believe what I'm seeing."

Allison pulled Tony into a tight hug. "I know. Thanks for helping me out. You went above and beyond the best friend with benefits duties. I don't think I can ever repay you."

Tony squeezed back. "You had my back when I was still in the closet and cursed out anyone who said I wasn't bi just confused. I've seen how much this hurt you and I wouldn't leave you to do this alone."

"Enough sappy junk you guys. Time to get to business." Blake teased, wiping sweat off her forehead. "I'm gonna wait outside. I've seen enough of all this stuff for a lifetime." She kissed Zinta on the cheek. "Come get me when you're done!" She called, trotting out of the chamber.

"Yes, let us begin." Velis purred, pressing against Tony's back, and slipped his warm hands around his cock. "If this is that last time we shall play, I want to make it special." The way he drew out every syllable made Tony gasp and hump into the hot, clawed hand.

Zinta pulled Allison into her arms, cupping Allison's breasts in both hands. "Perhaps when you are back home, we shall play again? I dare not deny Velis the much-deserved experience of your first orgasm but those after I would love to taste." A forked tongue slithered up Allison's neck before urging the human to meet her lips. Ali gratefully accepted, moaning into Zinta's mouth and shuddering in her arms.

"You should taste her, my friend. Just delectable." Velis continued to stroke Tony until his cock began to drip.

Zinta giggled and tugged Allison down to the warm floor with her. "Have a seat and let me see if Velis is correct." She purred, beckoning Ali to straddle her face.

Allison turned to give herself a chance to feast as well, taking a moment to draw in the ambrosial scent of the succubi's dripping folds before talking a long lick. She whined as a long tongue penetrated her; slithering around to gather as much of Ali's juices as she could and tease her clit.

"Isn't that beautiful?" Velis growled into Tony's ear before nipping at the lobe. When Tony whimpered, Velis stroked faster. "Go on. Join the fun."

Tony knelt above Zinta's head and squeezed Allison's ass in both hands. She looked back and nodded before going back to her meal.

As Tony slid deep inside her, Allison threw her head back and cried out in bliss. She arched her hips to take Tony to the hilt as Zinta licked at his balls.

"Let us not leave that pretty mouth idle." Velis moved to stand before Allison and lifted her chin. He pressed the tip of his cock against her lips and Ali opened wide and stuck out her tongue to draw him into the back of her throat.

Allison looked up at him as she worked the hot shaft into her throat, leaning into the clawed hand slithering into her hair but keeping her own pace as she bobbed her head. Velis groaned and his pleasure made Allison clench around Tony's cock; forcing a strained cry from his throat as he pumped faster.

"Yessssss." Velis sighed and Magesty hissed as Tony neared his release. Allison whimpered, shuddering through her frustration as Velis and Tony filled her from both ends. Velis caught Allison before she could fall, gathering the trembling woman up into his arms as the others recovered.

"I see." The leader walked up to Allison and wiped a tear from her cheek. "What a twisted trick of fate. But I believe I will be strong enough to overcome this."

Chapter Three

Majesty sent all but Velis and Ali away to clean themselves up while they discussed Alison's condition.

"Follow me." They said, and Ali gathered up her belongings to obey.

"They will not tell you their name," Velis whispered to Alison. "No being can know it otherwise They could be summoned at random."

"Any other protocol I need to know?" Allison's heart pounded and she hugged her bag tight as she walked.

"Just do what our leader says. Like me, They are trying to help you." Velis placed a kiss on her forehead. "Have no fear of this place, Allison. I would never let anything happen to you."

The heart-pounding nervousness turned into a hopeful flutter and Allison smiled. "Promise?"

Velis chuckled. "I swear, Allison."

Majesty took them to a private chamber with an enormous pool-sized to fit the leader's full form as They were taller than any other inhabitants of this realm. The pool was fed by steaming waterfalls of varying heights spilling from the high stone walls.

"Cleanse yourself in this area first then join me in the main bath." The leader turned before Allison could reply even if the beauty of this place left her slack jawed.

"I don't think I've ever seen anything so beautiful." Ali gasped as Velis lead her to bathe.

"Indeed. I have never been this far into the palace. Majesty seldom takes any being here."

"Wow." Allison kept staring but scolded herself for doing so.

"I shall allow you to bathe yourself this time." Velis nuzzled her neck and gave her bottom an encouraging smack. "As a short rest before Majesty instructs us."

Allison headed for a private area lit by glittering torches and crystals reflecting the light in a dazzling array of colors. A granite shower using a natural outcrop as the showerhead steamed with warm water and a neatly placed towel waited for her on a seat nearby. Allison left her clothes and bag near the bench and stepped into the stream of warm water with a sigh but that breath reminded her of Blake's warning about the air and washed quickly.

When she was done, Allison remained naked when she met Majesty and Velis already soaking in the grand pool. She hesitated at the sight of the pair of incubi waiting for her in the steaming pool

"Come now, Allison." Majesty's voice made Allison shudder with need and she carefully descended the stone stairs into the warm scented waters. "Velis, you may begin."

"This may be our last romp together, sweet one." He pressed his lips to hers and coaxed her into his arms. He teased her mouth open to entwine his tongue with hers. Ali reached around to cup his ass and bring his cock to rub against her.

"Turn her." Majesty leaned back against the side of the bath and stroked Their member to hardness.

Velis obeyed, sliding his cock against the crack of her ass and fondling her heaving breasts. "Are you ready, precious?" He teased her hole with the tip of his dripping shaft.

"Yes." She moaned, arching her back.

"Slowly." Majesty stood and pressed Allison's lips to Their dick. "She will need to drink."

Velis pumped his hips slowly, his claws digging into Ali's plump ass as he fought to keep control. "Yes, my liege." He growled.

Allison licked at the wet crown; the taste sweet and addictive. She reached up to cup Their balls and felt the moist slit behind it. She slipped two fingers inside, alternating with toying with Their balls causing Majesty to growl with pleasure.

A massive wet hand curled into her hair. "I can see why she fascinates you." Majesty's wings fluttered and Their hips moved to press deeper into Allison's throat.

Ali relaxed her jaw and pressed forward to suck harder, encouraged by the gentle press of the hand in her hair. She felt Velis' cock slowly stretching her open and hummed around the shaft in her throat.

"Hmmm... Good girl. Now, drink every drop down." Majesty croaked and Allison felt the shaft twitch in her mouth before it was filled with sugary sweet jizz.

Allison gulped down the thick, sugary liquid, reminded of every dessert she had ever enjoyed enough to lean back in her seat and close her eyes in bliss. But the delight here dwarfed them all.

"Faster, Velis." Majesty's voice shuddered as They came and Velis keened high in his throat and obeyed, his hips grinding against Ali's. She threw her head back as the last drip of the Majesty's seed slid down her throat. "Now. Finish now."

Velis lost control and pounded into Allison, causing her to cry out as Majesty held her above water. She clung to Majesty as she felt the familiar cresting of her bliss, clenching tight around Velis' cock. She braced for the usual gut-wrenching halt, the frustration of ecstasy cut cruelly short but then the sweet taste in her mouth from Majesty's cum spread over her entire body, warmth centering in her belly before it exploded. Fire burst in her veins and Allison let loose a scream of relief that echoed through the stone walls. Her vision turned white, her muscles burned, and the force of her first orgasm left her breathless. She heard Velis howl behind her as she weakly collapsed in Majesty's arms.

After a few surreal moments, Majesty lifted Allison from the pool. "Your contract is fulfilled and your summoner is healed. It is time for her and the rest of your guests to return home."

"Y-yes my liege." Velis whispered, following his leader on shaking legs, as if drunk on the potency of his meal.

CHAPTER FOUR

After another trip through the portal which Allison barely remembered in the haze of finally attaining an orgasm to feed Velis - who ate greedily - she came back to herself as Tony drove her home. She insisted on her stability and Tony left her alone in her home.

'*It's too quiet.*' She thought leaning against the arm of her couch. Allison hugged her bag and fell backward on the cushions, staring at the ceiling. Her muscles ached and her forehead tingled with the vague memory of a final kiss goodbye.

"Ugh, don't be weepy." She said to herself. "He held up his end of the deal and had to go home. Simple as that." Ali stood and went for her bedroom to strip off her dusty clothes and toss them into her hamper. When she went to shake out the clothes in her bag, the dust made her sneeze, and all the contents scattered on the floor. Something hard hit her foot with a thunk.

"Shit!" She dropped the bag and reached down to rub her aching foot. Ali ruffled through the clothes to find out whatever item left a forming bruise on her skin and uncovered the black stone obelisk.

"He didn't take it." She gasped, wrapping both hands around it. Without hesitation, Allison spoke the words to make the stone glow once more.

"Ah, we meet once again, lovely lady." Velis sauntered through a vortex of light and bent to cup her chin in his hand. "I would be terribly remiss in my duties if I did not follow up on my work."

Blinking against the blinding light, Allison smiled. "Let's test drive then!"

Velis scooped Ali in his arms, his cock already rising. "And I shall not leave until I am sure our cure has fully taken hold."

The end.

Don't miss out!

Visit the website below and you can sign up to receive emails whenever Cassandra Vayne publishes a new book. There's no charge and no obligation.

https://books2read.com/r/B-A-UTYE-NVDLB

BOOKS 2 READ

Connecting independent readers to independent writers.

Did you love *Incubus Dreams: Complete Collection*? Then you should read *Fylgja*[1] by Cassandra Vayne!

[2]

While diligently working late at a veterinary office, Thaddeus steps in to save a raccoon from being mauled to death by a starving stray dog. After tranquilizing both, he turns to find the raccoon is gone and a naked stranger is in its place.

Read more at https://cassandravaynebooks.blogspot.com/.

---

1. https://books2read.com/u/boYdyZ

2. https://books2read.com/u/boYdyZ

Also by Cassandra Vayne

Incubus Dreams
Incubus Dreams: Part 1
Incubus Dreams: Part 2
Incubus Dreams: Part 3
Incubus Dreams: Part 4
Incubus Dreams: Complete Collection

Standalone
Good Boy
Fylgja
The Inheritance
Prey
Ink and Pom-Poms
A Flash of Scale
Trail Run
Forest's Patience: A Paranormal Lesbian Romance
A Dance for the Warlord

About the Author

A woman full of naughty dreams who can't help but put them to paper. Sign up for release news and more at this link: http://eepurl.com/db7uTD

Read more at https://cassandravaynebooks.blogspot.com/.